The Scarecrow

In a far away town called Hack-on-Wield

A lone scarecrow stood in a farmer's field.

His clothes were all tatters, his hat was all torn;

His job was to keep the crows from the corn.

He was stuffed full of straw
in his arms and his legs;

Instead of fingers he had wooden pegs.

Indeed, he looked quite a miserable sight,

Stuck high on a pole all day and all night.

The scarecrow's name was Old Fuzzy Fred,

Because of the straw that stuck out of his head.

But Fred was **unhappy**, he felt terribly sad;

There wasn't a friend in the world that he had.

Each person who passed the field of corn,

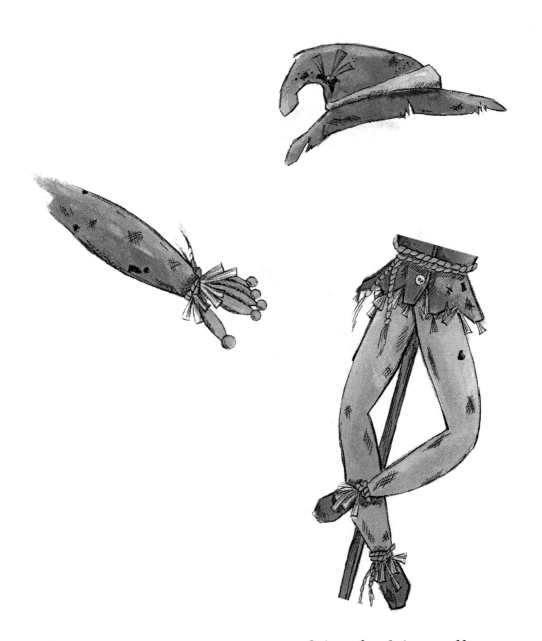

Would see Fuzzy Fred with his clothing all torn,

And they'd **shriek** at the sight of this scary man,

They'd hide in the bushes, and some of them ran.

With no one to talk to, no friend at all,

Poor Fuzzy Fred was alone, standing tall.

He looked down at the world stretched out below,

And down his straw face, tears started to flow.

Then one day a crow
flew down on his head.

'Hey, why are you crying?' the black crow said.

'Because I'm **alone**, and I'm tattered and torn,

And all I do is stare out at this corn.'

`I scare all the crows, all the people, too—`

And then he stopped. 'But I don't scare you.'

'Oh, no,' cawed the bird. 'You don't scare me.

But I've just flown in from the city, you see.

'In a city there's plenty
more scary than you.

That's why I'm brave.
Now here's what I'll do:

I'll call every day and we'll have a chat.

And I won't eat the corn...
                Now, how about that?'

'Oh, would you?
Oh, thank you!'
cried Fuzzy Fred.

'A friend of my own, perched up on my head!'

At last Fred was happy, he wasn't alone.

Now there was no reason for him to moan.

Now everyone passing the field of corn

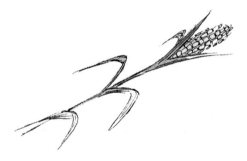

Looked at the scarecrow all tattered and torn.

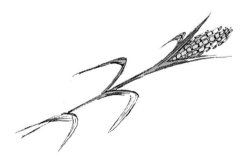

They laughed right out loud, and one of them said,

'Look at the crow on the scarecrow's head!'

'He's supposed to be scary,' a small boy said,

'But he doesn't frighten that crow on his head.

In fact, they look friendly. It just goes to show:

He is a scarecrow

that can't scare a crow!'

This is the second book by GINA THOMPSON who started writing stories for her own children when they were young. She continues to use her own stories in her work with vulnerable children and uses ryhme to communicate feelings and emotions. She lives and works in Keighley, West Yorkshire.

DATE DUE			

GAYLORD

LaVergne, TN USA
03 January 2011

210774LV00007B/88/A